This Little Tiger Book Belongs To:

_____

_____

_____

_____

_____

For Lucy and Ruben, with love
— D.H.
For Tim and Noah
— J.C.

LITTLE TIGER PRESS
An imprint of Magi Publications
1 The Coda Centre, 189 Munster Road. London SW6 6AW
www.littletigerpress.com
This paperback edition published in 2001
First published in Great Britain 2001
Text © 2001 Diana Hendry • Illustrations © 2001 Jane Chapman
Diana Hendry and Jane Chapman have asserted their rights
to be identified as the author and illustrator of this work
under the Copyright, Designs and Patents Act, 1988.
Printed in Italy • All rights reserved
ISBN 1 85430 759 2 •   5 7 9 10 8 6 4

The Very Busy Day

Diana Hendry

Jane Chapman

LITTLE TIGER PRESS

London

It was a hot sunny day, and Big Mouse was digging in the garden.

SWISH!

Little Mouse sat on the swing, wearing his sun hat. "There's a lot of digging to do," said Big Mouse. "Come and help me, Little Mouse." "I'm too busy to help," said Little Mouse. "I'm dreaming up something." And he swung up and down, up and down.

"You could put in these seeds," said
Big Mouse. "If you plant them in
the dark, they'll dream up flowers."

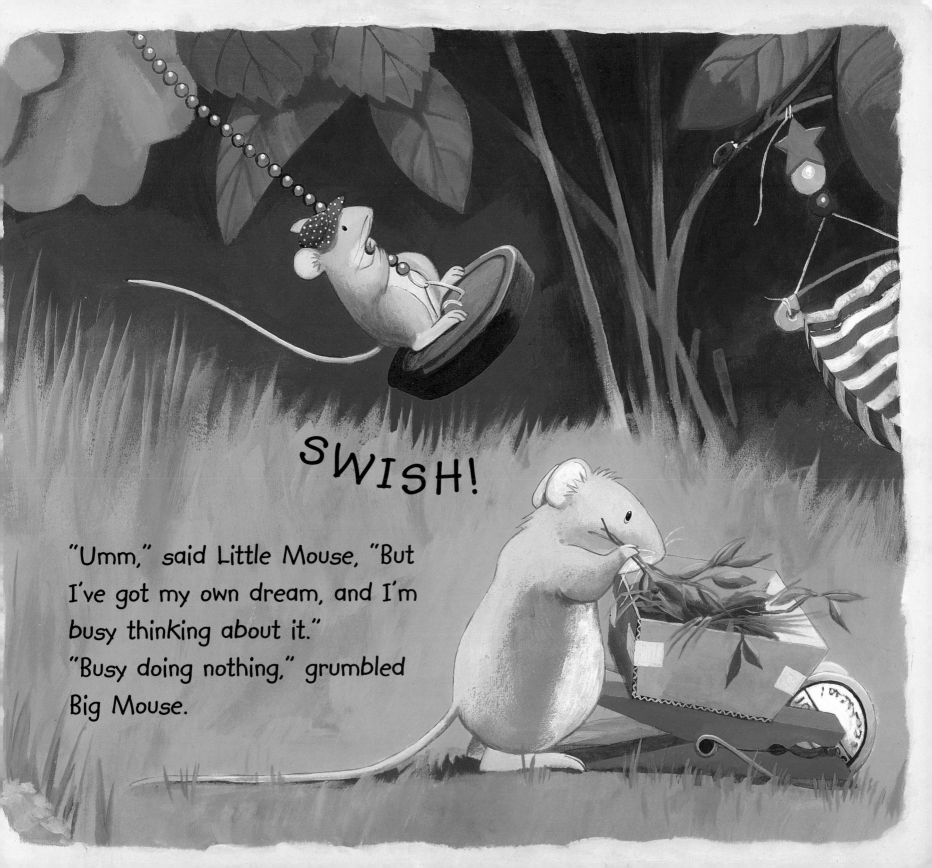

SWISH!

"Umm," said Little Mouse, "But I've got my own dream, and I'm busy thinking about it."
"Busy doing nothing," grumbled Big Mouse.

WHEEE!

Little Mouse slid off the swing and jumped into the wheelbarrow. He lay and gazed at the sky. "I need that wheelbarrow for the weeds," said Big Mouse. "And look at all the mess you've made."

Big Mouse tipped Little Mouse
out on to the grass. "Please,
Little Mouse, I need some help."
"I'm far too busy to help," cried
Little Mouse, and he ran off to
pick some daisies.

Big Mouse picked up all the
weeds. He mopped his brow
and rubbed his back.
"Phew, it's hot," he puffed . . .

"And this barrow's very heavy all of
a sudden."
It was heavy because Little Mouse
had jumped back in! He was sitting on
top of the weeds making a daisy chain.

"I'm not pushing you and the weeds," said Big Mouse indignantly. "Out you get! Come and help me take the weeds to the rubbish dump." Little Mouse hung the daisy chain round his neck and scrambled out of the barrow.

But he didn't help
Big Mouse. He picked
lots and lots of clover
instead. He put the
clover in a flowerpot
on the back doorstep.

HUFF!

PUFF!

Big Mouse pushed the wheelbarrow to
the dump by himself, muttering crossly.

Big Mouse went to find his rake.
He couldn't see Little Mouse anywhere.
"Come on, Little Mouse," he called.
"There's a little rake here
for you too."

As Big Mouse climbed down the ladder, Little Mouse poked his head out. "Can't you see I'm busy?" he called. "I'm collecting birds' feathers. This dream is very hard work." "Humph!" said Big Mouse. "There's dreaming and there's doing. What about a little doing from you!"

Little Mouse had found three
snowy white feathers.
He laid them carefully
on the doorstep.

By now, Big Mouse was busy. "Little Mouse," he called. "You could help me carry this strawberry down the ladder." "Can't stop now," said Little Mouse. "I need something from the kitchen."

The sun had made Big
Mouse's head ache, and he
felt very snappy with Little
Mouse for not helping him.
"Whatever's he doing now?"
he grumbled.

Little Mouse rushed out into the garden. "Big Mouse, Big Mouse," he called. "Look what I've made for you!

It's your very own special sun hat!"
"Oh thank you, Little Mouse," said
Big Mouse, putting it on his head.
"Now I can see why you've been
so busy dreaming. It's my very
special Dream Hat!"

"We've both been very busy,"
said Little Mouse, yawning.
"There's just time to do one
more thing," said Big Mouse.

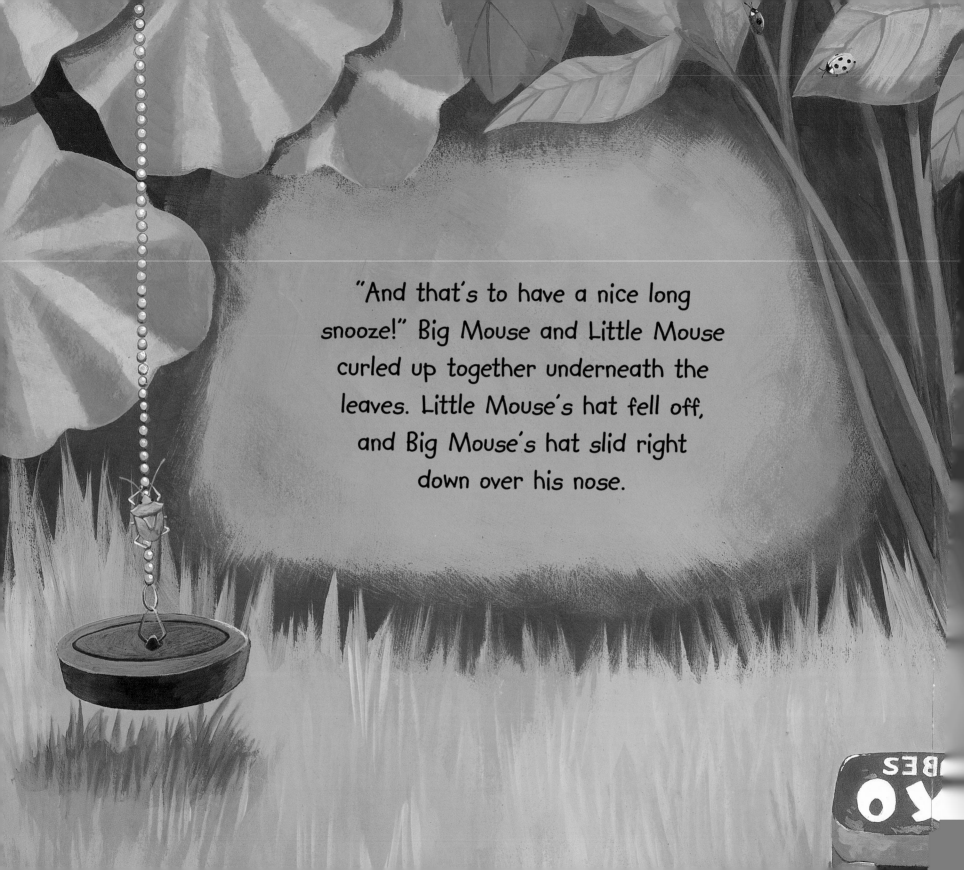

"And that's to have a nice long snooze!" Big Mouse and Little Mouse curled up together underneath the leaves. Little Mouse's hat fell off, and Big Mouse's hat slid right down over his nose.

Titus's Troublesome Tooth

LINDA JENNINGS AND GWYNETH WILLIAMSON

Hang about

for

Wait for me, Little Tiger!

Julie Sykes · Tim Warnes

more books by

Little Tiger Press

JULIE SYKES · JACK TICKLE

Little Rocket's Special Star

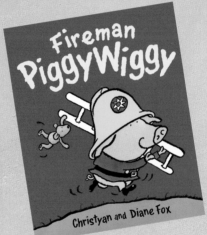

Fireman PiggyWiggy

Christyan and Diane Fox

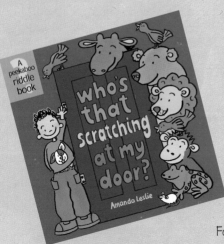

A peekaboo riddle book

who's that scratching at my door?

Amanda Leslie

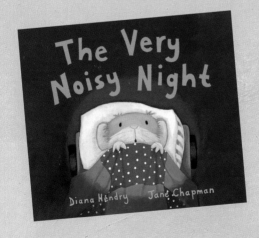

The Very Noisy Night

Diana Hendry · Jane Chapman

Little Mouse and the Big Red Apple

A.H. Benjamin and Gwyneth Williamson

For information regarding any of the above titles or for our catalogue, please contact us at:
Little Tiger Press, 1 The Coda Centre, 189 Munster Road, London SW6 6AW, UK
Tel: 020 7385 6333 • Fax: 020 7385 7333 • e-mail: info@littletiger.co.uk • www.littletigerpress.com